◆

In the mouth of a blue whale, there is somebody who has set up camp, humming low echoes into the walls of the whale's belly, knocking bones against harpstring baleen. It is the Sea Impervious. It is the drinking well in the center of the city. It is the Fool's Ocean. It is anywhere.

Once upon a time there was a homeless heart.

Homeless hearts are like broken blues riffs, like single drum beats, like pieces of words begging for bodies, for places to hold their weight, full of messages erupted from whispers. Homeless hearts nestle into the cradles of coral and coal. They become caught again and again, a bass drum muscle. Homeless hearts in seas pump water but are hungry for blood.

This is the beginning.

The beginning is about something too old to be named, building
from bones and bits of jellyfish, a body for the heart, a body with
ribs and fingers and two eyes and a throat full of songs.

The beginning is about the creature opening her mouth and
laughing, about The Nameless cautioning her of many things, but
most of all, of her jellyfish skin, like layers of water paper and
dreams, fragile.

The beginning is full of beginnings, each lonelier than the last. This is
a story about falling in love.
But for falling, there must be gravity. And for a true and barbaric
gravity, one must eventually leave the water.

This is a story about gravity. Truly, all stories are eventually about
gravity.

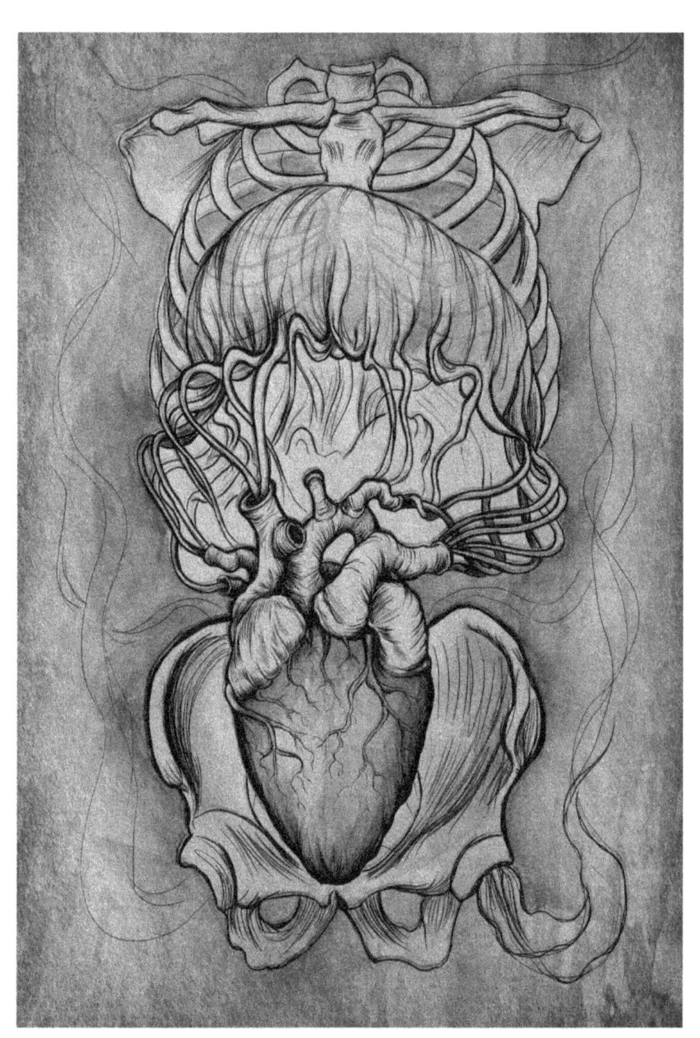

◆

A Found Letter Inside a Bundle by a Bed Roll and Candles in
the Tunnels Beneath the Temple of Condition. Present Day.

44 23 15 41 45 15 15 33 24 43 11 31 24 51 15.
52 15 21 11 24 31 15 14. 31 15 15 44 32 15.
21 34 45 33 14 42 54. 34 33 15 23 34 45 42.
11=A 44=T 15=E

◆

A Found Letter Inside a bundle by a Bed Roll and Candles in
the Tunnels Beneath the Temple of Condition. Present Day.

My Reluctant Love,
I am afraid of the city. I have never been afraid of the city.

Some tide is turning here, I don't know what. When you left
for the continent, I worried for you. There are days
where I hate you. Where I know whatever atrocity
has likely fallen you, you have done it to yourself.
Sometimes I wonder if you have gone there just to be
somewhere as terrible as you are. It's as though
whatever darkness lives inside you cannot be
matched. Like you're full of something ugly and you
can't survive unless you are someplace that feeds it.
Some days I think you even tried to consume me,
but maybe this is just how you are. All I know is
that you are gone, you used to be here. All I know is
you did not leave until I finally believed you would
not. There are days when I hate you, it's true, but
wondering where you are is worse.

I don't know if I even wonder why you left. I used to.
Sometimes I can't remember how long you've been
gone. Two years? Three? Where are you?

Since the establishment took the city states of the continent
down below, the merchants have become more and

more uneasy. Now the Outland Queen has a price on her head. Our age of queens ended a thousand years ago here in The Floating City, but down there, it's just now ending. Maybe. I don't know. I stopped trading in the markets on the continent after you left. I stopped because I kept looking for you. I stopped because I found your face in every face. I stopped because my breath kept catching, because I kept willing you to arrive. Imagining you standing in front of me, half drunk, boring into me with those rich earth-colored eyes, smirking. Imagining you asking to trade for a bell. I stopped bringing bells to the market and it is your fault and I don't know how to forgive you for it.

Now I am learning to make them. I am apprenticing with an old bellfounder. He does not speak much. When I began learning from him, he didn't really speak to me at all. I just had to watch. I asked so many questions, and instead of answering any of them, he'd just keep working. I'd have to watch for the answers.

Do you know how a bell is cast? Most people in The Floating City do, I suppose. We are a city full of bells. You cast it with a mould. But tuning the bell, that is something only the bellfounders seem to know about. I suppose it's a thing you don't think about until you are doing it yourself. My whole life in the city, even when I was a bell merchant, the bells just were. I knew what they were made from, I knew where they were made, but I never asked what made them sing.

You tune the bell by taking parts of it away after it is already cast. You do this with a lathe. It is the most difficult thing I have ever done. Every movement, every breath, it's a measurement. One slip, one imprecise calculation, and the whole thing is ruined. Maybe it is not ruined, maybe it just turns out different. But when you have a specification as to what the bell should sound like, and you remove too much from the lip, there is no coming back. You have a completely different bell. I have a whole room full of

*accident bells. You would be terrible at this, you
were always too cocky for measurements.*

*We have been making bells here for as long as anyone knows,
bells everywhere. Do you remember how you once
told me you knew the story of the first bell in the city
and then would not say what it was? I wish I did
not remember. You haunt everything, even the bells.
Even my hands making the bells. My whole, stupid,
foolish heart. My heart is probably a bell.*

*What scares me most is that there is no longer any safe place.
Maybe this doesn't concern you anymore. Maybe you
have the wasting sickness down on the continent.
Maybe you are dead. Ten years, it has been, and The
Establishment only becomes stronger. When will
they come here? They cannot stay away forever. If
they do, will the city survive? I don't know. What is
surviving?*

*There is a tension building. The specters are beginning
to...well, they are beginning to notice us. It sounds
utterly mad when I say it, but they just are. I locked
eyes with one the other day. My eyes met his and he
saw me. He really, really saw me. For as long as I've
been alive, for as long as my grandaddy even has
been alive, for as long as anyone I know has been
alive, the specters went about their business in the
city as though they didn't know we were here. Like
we were specters in their city. What does it mean if
they know we are here? Will they speak to us? Where
do they come from? Last year, an alchemist
disappeared. Just vanished. They say he was
looking for the origin of the specters.*

*And the clockworks, they are beginning to notice us, too. The
machinists say they are at a loss for why the beasts
are gaining such vivid sentience, but no one believes
the machinists. The professors at the Lyceum are
divided on how they feel about this business, and
the disagreements are becoming heated. There is
unease everywhere. Like a crawling storm. It's fear.
It's permeating all the people.*

These days it feels like the only thing that is not fragile is the clown who wanders the bazaar every day. Everything else is shifting, but the clown is steady. The clown and I have never spoken, but I find a deep comfort in watching them. How long has the clown been here? Nobody knows. Nobody pays the clown any mind. Maybe when the city finally collapses on itself from the weight of empires or fear, maybe that clown will still be there.

Are we being punished for losing our own history? All these years, we have taken for granted that The Floating City holds itself above the Lost Continent, that the five moons move around us all, that the mechanics will build and repair the airships, that the sun will come, that the water will run, that we will sleep in our beds. We should have known when The Establishment came to the continent that we were not safe. We should have known that it was only a matter of time, that it is when everything continues as normal that one must be most cautious. Instead, we just made our bells.

What is next, will the bells ring themselves? Will the specters and the clockworks unite to kill us, or worse? What if The Establishment could harness them as tools? What if The Establishment discovers there is no queen? That we are rulerless? That we are beginning to divide against each other? That we are fools?

I am afraid. I am afraid and you are not here. And if something awful happens, will it happen without my ever knowing if you survived it? Without my ever ringing a bell at the burning of your body?

I don't know where to send this letter. I just love you. And I can never forgive you. I am afraid for the city. There is no one to tell. You are gone.

Relenting,
Elábrándozik

◆

A Found Letter Inside a Bundle by a Bed Roll and Candles in the Tunnels Beneath the Temple of Condition. Present day.

Master Willows,

I hope this letter finds you. In the event that it doesn't, I've set up an alchemic enchantment on the lettering paper by linking a cibustine binding with a piece of your hair.

At first, I didn't think much of the hair I found on the message you left for me in the Archives. I found another one in the first 10 pages of The Interior Design of Older Times, and then another one in Great Queens: Myth or Matter. I thought maybe you had started going bald. When I got notice you'd taken a sudden leave of absence, I became worried. I found more hair in A Detailed History of Lake Bromst.

Many curious and strange things have happened since you've left. I've made much progress with my glass. I keep it on a necklace. It feels quite content to look around at something other than the bottom of the lake.

Something happened to Sivvy, the Cartography of Anomaly student. Rumors were dancing around about how he was running late to an exam and tried to take a shortcut down an alley and ended up back in his room, penniless with none of his possessions, not even his shoelaces. Some thought he was drunk, or sleep walking, or that a specter got him.

Then I had a long night, like many I've had before in the Archives, chasing books around the stacks and reading them for as long as they'd stay still. I left as the sun began to touch the horizon and went for a delirious wander back to my room.

The sun was rising lilac as I emerged into a plaza as beautiful as a meadow. I'd never been to this part of

the Lyceum. I heard Master Drell in my head,
saying there are places in our city you can only find
if they want to be found.

The trees were sparse, but tall and full, and the ground was
full of flowers and ferns. The air smelled of warm
cardamom and honey. A flurry of movement pulled
my eyes to a tent in the heart of the garden and I felt
the blue glass flutter against my chest.
What happened next I can only describe as becoming the
glass. I did not hide, but stood extraordinarily still.
Sivvy came out of the tent, holding something
wrapped in a piece of light cloth. If he looked at me,
he didn't see me. I don't think he could have.
I followed him in a way I've never moved before. I moved the
way a ship glides through dark water. I moved the
way the wind carries over the plains. I moved the
way sunlight cuts through mist in the harbor. I
didn't make a sound.

Far from the garden, Sivvy sat down on a bench and opened
the parcel. In his hands he held a thick bronze
compass. It rather looked like a motor. It had many
moving parts, all inscribed in a language I didn't
recognize. But I wasn't me. I was the glass. The
glass recognized the language.

The glass also realized the significance of what Sivvy was
holding. It was something called an orbisium, and
whoever knows it's name can ask it where anything
is. Anything. An orbisium is capable of revealing
where all things are, both tangible and intangible.
Both waking and asleep. A very powerful tool.

It was made of metal, wrapped in leather and cotton and
whispers. It was inscribed with an ordinary pen by
an extraordinary hand. All of this I know because
the glass knows.

As we left Sivvy, the glass showed me parts of the orbisium
were all of the things Sivvy was missing when he
had his incident: leather from his purse, cotton from
his shoelaces, the metal it was cast from, his coins.
Far from the garden, and far from Sivvy, the glass

*First, the glass told me she was the Queen's perfume of heart,
and though we were far away I suddenly smelled
warm cardamom and honey.*

*Second, the glass told me there was only one person who
could craft an orbisium that delicate with only so
few things binding it together. The Queen.*

*I haven't had a chance to talk to Sivvy yet. And I haven't
been able to find that little garden again. My glass
has been reluctant to tell me any new secrets.*

*But I've been thinking of the orbisium, and all of the things
it could lead me to. The secret of the specters. Where
Wart disappeared to. I could find a trove of hidden
treasures.*

I could find you, if you need finding.

*Write back if you can. I know you can look after yourself, but
I'd be lying if I said I weren't gravely worried.*

Your student,

Camille of Shattered Glass

♦

A page Torn from a Book Retrieved from the Hollow of a Tree
in the Lyceum Courtyard, A Proverb, Date of Original
Publication Suspected to be Prior to the Age of Queens.

*And the youth stood upon the grasping oak roots, shouting a
word to the descending sky, a name to end all that is. For it
is known that no power shall be unthroned until it is so
named.*

**Commentary, handwritten

"Mortals think death is a matter of rending flesh, of dividing blood from bone. It is sssssilliness born of children who have known the world as formed from ticking visssscera. Our breaths are quickened of ideas, of the words and hearts that fessssster up from passssssion's roots. It's there, like a poisssson, in all of their tales, all of their movements and dreamssss, and they cannot see it. They risssse up and proclaim righteous the deaths in the name of...whatever fool thing they can imagine. But the truth is the assssp's bite: It is the name that kills. Even the most hidden enemy cannot ressssist the toll of their name, the key to their unmaking. A moment on the lipsssss is a dagger in the heart."

Such is my witness to the last(?) cursed words of the flame, yet unnamed

---Knight Jacinth of the 4th Untamed Battalion

♦

A Found Letter from the Archives of the Stewards [Artifact 705: a scroll tucked into the underside of the stairwell of a brothel], Dated Ten Years Following the Execution.

I knew the Queen.
I knew her when she meant well and I knew her when she
        was a monster.

The Queen was a song in the time of gods and devils. She
        was born in the water. She had no body. She was
        only a single heart retched unceremoniously from
        the inside of an oyster. At the center of her heart
        lived a pearl nestled in the left ventricle.

I knew the Queen after she emerged from the sea on shaky
        legs into the hot sun, wearing sand-toughened skin.
        I knew the Queen when she was naked and wet and
        shivering and learning what gravity was. I knew
        the Queen when she told the story of her bargain
        with The Nameless, how she agreed to give them the

*pearl in her heart for passage onto the shore. How
she inhaled the salt air into her lungs. How they left
the pearl there and said they would take it someday,
but not now.*

Not now.

Someday, but not now.

*I knew that the Queen loved birds. During her years alone,
wandering the continent, she learned her songs from
the birds, curled her tongue and pushed air from
her lungs, she did not sound like them, but she
learned the pitches and found rhythms in rocks and
trees and she learned what her throat could do.
From the found bodies of expired birds, she took the
bones, cleaned them, tied them into her hair.*

*I knew that when she came upon The City of Towers on the
Lost Continent, she begged in the streets telling
fortunes with the bones she kept in her hair. I knew
the Queen while she learned about currency, about
coins and gems and things that could be traded for
other things. I knew the Queen when she first tasted
fermented drinks, when she parted her teeth and
sang her wild songs for drunk tavern patrons. When
she learned what her throat could do.*

*I knew the Queen when she learned what a body was. She
learned about bodies when she discovered her own
body, wanted and wanting. When she learned what
it was to exchange her hands and mouth and thighs
for coins which she exchanged for food and clothing
and blankets and beds and oils to massage into the
skin of her arms and face and feet.*

*When she took what was left over and gave it away to
whomever needed it, I knew the Queen when she
was worried about the people who could not afford
to eat.*

*I knew the Queen when she discovered what a tambourine
was.*

When she danced until her feet bled.

*When the people who loved her began to call her Queen of
Bones, for all the bones that lived in her hair.*

When she learned what her throat could do.

*I knew the Queen when she was a ghost in a story that was
not a ghost story, just a story with a ghost in it.*

I knew the Queen when she wrote poems.

No one knew the Queen.

*One thousand years ago, I was at the Queen's execution. I
was the only one who wept.*

◆

I do not know when I arrived.

There is a story they tell. It is about how I was a whore. But I had been here so long, by then, time felt like a crawling breeze. When I arrived in Floating City, it was after years on The Lost Continent. When I arrived, they loved me. When I arrived, I loved them back.

The Little Queen/ Once a pauper
Rode in on a noble's offer
Slit his throat/ and drank his blood
Won't rest/ till we're all bottoms-up

The Little Queen's/ own lullaby
The sound of cracking bones at night
Should your roses/ ever whisper
A warning/ that she binds you hither
The Little Queen is thirsty, always thirsty

Sometimes I hum the song in my sleep and wake up humming it. Sometimes I think the song is a prayer. I have asked many people over the years, who will love you when you are wicked? They always come up with a list. It is their mothers, their siblings, their children. I have none of these. Does this mean no one will love me when I am wicked?

In the days of slaves, she was unbound.

The slaves in Floating City came from the nomadic clans who roamed The Lost Continent, but it was not their bodies that were enslaved, it was their spirits. The slaves were apparition-like, person-forms, ghostly creatures that did their masters' bidding. Ordinary bidding. People who built fires in the winter, kept the draperies from being dusty, made the food, and threw the wasted food away. Translucent-ish, but apparent as your or I. They were real enough to touch. Poppets, they were called, or Bone People. They made sounds like flesh people did, carried things, held things. They spoke in mild, agreeable tones, but their eyes were boiling, always boiling. Like angry volcano hearts. She used to think of them as the Volcano People.

Only the noble families had Bone People, and only the families' house alchemists knew how these apparitions were formed, how they were controlled, where their bodies were. At night, children would frighten each other with stories of loosed Bone People, named so ironically because they had no bones. *Mind your lessons, or the chemist will make you a Bone Person,* nannies would threaten to incorrigible littles.

There were not any flesh-and-blood clanspeople in the city. Only the spirits of them, held by devils or men no one but a certain few alchemists knew.

When she arrived, she drifted among the workers, through the Foundry District, waking and sleeping against the hammer and iron sounds, through the taverns, among the clockmakers and machinists and smiths and pirates and songworkers and in the courtyards of the temples. Everywhere. Anywhere. She slept in a room above a tavern. She sang songs and spilled poems for drinkers and thieves and laborers. She told stories of the continent. She told stories of the sea.

She was beautiful and her songs were an open wound. Her songs were sharp like new teeth. Her songs were cold air on bare skin. She sang her way through the taverns, she sang her way across dark streets and bedsheets, and she sang her way into the bed of a man wealthy enough to keep her in the west wing of his own home.

Somewhere in this sprawling estate, there was a wife. There were children. But every affluent home had rooms for mistresses.

There were six noble families who ruled the city together, none of whose names she bothered to learn. Even the one who gifted her mechanical peacocks and embroidered gowns and pearls, who called her his Queen of Bones as he held himself above her on silk sheets nightly. She did not learn his name, either. To speak a thing's name gives it power. She called him so many things. She called him her Tower. She called him her Fortress. She called him her Master. All things he believed were words of endearment. Never did she speak his name.

And she had no name for him to speak. She was only the Queen of Bones, a title tossed at her feet in streets by drunk sailors.

In the City, rumors spread among the families about one of their own capturing the Queen of Bones. Rumors spread among the taverns and in the streets of the Bone Queen selling herself for greener pastures. She was a traitor or a trickster, depending on who carried the tale. At dinners and socials at the nobleman's palace, even his wife would take part in delightedly parading a finely dressed Queen of Bones before their guests, polished and pristine but with the bones still in her hair. By request-which-was-really-command, she would dance, she would sing, she would earn her silks and picture windows and thick wool rugs. *Look,* they would say, *the city has a Queen, and she is ours.* While every noble family had a small palace, and every palace housed mistresses, this was the only one that kept the Queen of

Bones. In a society whose noble class boasted a lifestyle based on the luxuries of specter servants and avant-garde machines, a live, tangible, breathing pet was a novelty.

She could have left any time. Instead she remained, a flesh-and-blood puppet, a traitor to a people she did not even come from, a people who claimed her anyway, a people she once claimed. She had been with them so long, the workers, peasants, that they believed she had been born of them. They forgot that she had come from nowhere. That she had just merely arrived. That she had no people. That it never did make her love them less. But now they went hungry while she ate honey spun by mechanical bees created by machinists in the Menageries. They slept in dirt while she feigned pleasured sighs on pressed sheets that were soft like cornsilk. She smiled through gritted teeth while sipping fermented fruit wine, while dancing for the families, while singing like a pet bird.

It was unlike her to be anybody's pet bird.

♦

A Found Letter Inside an Outer Pocket of a Discarded Wool Jacket In the Tunnels Beneath the Temple of Condition. Present day.

To Whom It May Concern,

Today after a lecture in the Lyceum I saw a group of students in a bit of what seemed to be a quarrel. I approached the group and saw they were reassembling simple clockwork beasts. They seemed agitated, which was odd, as all of the beasts were happily reassembled and going about being beasts. The students seemed distressed and I inquired as to what was the matter. Instead of a reply, one brave soul gathered one of the clockworks up. It was a tiny bird-like one. The student soothed it and proceeded to carefully remove a wing and place the gears, screws and wing parts on the ground. The student then set the bird down and took a few unsteady steps back. The creature looked to the student, and then the rest of the people gathered. Instead of waiting to be repaired the creature hopped up and started picking up the pieces of itself. It made a dinging chirpy noise and the other beasts came over and helped it attend to its injury.

In a matter of moments the creature was whole once more with no help from any of the students or myself. Once the thing was put right, all the beasts went back to doing their normal functions as if they hadn't just essentially performed a surgery on their companion.

We assert that the things taught here are completely understood to their innermost core. I fear however that we know far less of the things we cohabitate with in this city. I have heard from others that the specters are also behaving strangely. They have been seen gathering together as if in a discourse. They are seen without books roaming about in districts that are not their own.

I try my utmost to be logical person, but I can't explain the goings on of the city to myself, much less to students. I fear that I am paying more mind to rumor and relying less on my own knowledge of the things I have taught here for years. Is there a swell in the magic of all things in our land? Is the explained trying to out-pace our explanations?

I have heard people from the other districts are also experiencing inexplicable goings on. I hear more talk of the Queen, of the continent, and of those lost and found in the desert. How do I continue to teach in a world that just doesn't make sense to me any longer? What do I tell the others around me who look for answers when I am just as mystified?

I don't know if I look to you for answers or reassurance. In the end, I feel that this is something that we need to address. Not just for our peace of mind, but for the city as a whole.

Respectfully,

Althazar
Professor of Intents and Imaginations

◆

I was not captured by the noble family. I went willingly, through the front door. I was invited and I arrived. They put out tea for me, served me small cakes on thin glass plates, instructed their Bone People to show me to my rooms. And I stayed. But I neither arrived nor remained for the man who kept me.

I stayed for the alchemist, whose name I did learn, whose name I will never say again. It does not matter what small names we gave each other. It does not matter that the naming of something is a holy act. The dearest form of worship. A thing only reserved for kin and lovers and adversaries. It does not matter what sonnets he composed for my upturned wrists, or the way he clutched them in his sleep.

It does matter, though. It matters very much.

Maybe it even matters that he found me first, after midnight in a tavern, reciting a poem to a room full of blacksmiths well in their cups. The smiths loved poems because poems and songs are much like bending hot iron. There is a dance inside of it. They are the same thing, full of heat and soot and metal shavings. And when he asked my name, I did not tell him, because I did not have a name. I was the Queen of Bones because I was called that, traveled upward from the continent, to a city with no queens. Being called something is not at all like being named something.

When he asked for another poem, I gave it to him. And then another, and another, until all my poems were escaped breaths and fingertips and the shuffle of buttons escaping their latches, and he had a wife, but I had a mandolin.

And when I sang, his stories climbed out of him like old hope and kudzu, and he asked where my home was, and I did not tell him, because I had no home. And because I had no home, it was easy to find a home in the cradle of his body curled against mine. And because I imagined myself asleep in a home, it was easy to want it. In spite of his estranged wife somewhere below on The Lost Continent, the mystery of his tenure with the noble family he worked for, the strangeness of his work, I wanted it. In spite of the fact that to be nearer to him, I would have to go to the palace where he lived and worked. I would have to become his employer's whore. I still wanted it.

We can never escape what we love. It roots itself in us, makes us wild and untenable. It puts hooks in our ribs and makes puppets of us. Turns our ankles and wrists at its bidding. Holds us hostage.

How did he open me like a spring slide box? How many months did I let him pluck me like a gilded harp, how long was it? How many times did he wake with my hair in his mouth? How did he make me spill?

In the dark she would feel her way through the corridors after all the lights had gone out. She carried no lantern, in part to avoid being noticed, but most of all because she liked finding her way in the dark. Down flights of stairs, down into the laboratory. Down among the jars and vials and volumes of books. Amid the inkwells and animal teeth and glass carafes and work tables. To the fireplace in the study and the thick wool rug. Where he would trace the shapes of her ribs and jawline. Where he would unbraid her hair. Where she would sing him songs she learned on the continent.

"You are the moon," he would say.
"There are five moons. Which one am I?"
"The one that stays."
"None of them stay."

If there were nobody left in all the world who knew your name, would you remember it yourself? Would you search for it in the mouths of strangers, breaking open their lilts and syllables like sabra fruits? Would you study the hands of lovers as they undressed you, watching, waiting for the moment they would know it, or you would know it, or somebody would know it, hoping it would escape from spent breath, skipping over tongues? Would you be sure you could recognize it if it happened? What would you do if it did?

It was on her back atop the wool rug with her hands in his hair that she told him about the pearl in her heart. *A sixth moon,* he said. A sixth moon. And he became fixed on this tiny moon placed there by The Nameless. *How long ago,* he wanted to know. *How did you come from the sea? How did you live there? Who made you?* But questions are not built for answers. Questions are built for hanging in the air, between breaths, for holding you steady while you wait. Questions do not need answers. They need snake charmers, open windows, rivers.

Answers are just handfuls of sand.

Are names a thing you are born with? All these years, I watched them being given to people. What if it is not like that? What if your name belongs to you upon birth, and it is the job of your parents to see it and know it and say it first. What if names aren't given, what if they are always there? Where do they live, then? What part of a person houses their name? Where does it sleep? What does it dream?

If a name goes too long without being spoken, does it get sick? Does it die?

It was the most prestigious of the alchemists who worked for the families. Whether they were best at their craft was debatable, but they had to at least be clever. In the Alchemists Quarter, these positions were either coveted or looked upon with disdain, depending on how one thought of the nobility. Not everyone approved of the power the families held. Not everyone believed in the rulership of the wealthy. In fact, some believed the division of classes was amoral. Some believed there would come a day where the workers would be freed from rulership.

So when the Queen of Bones killed the noble family who housed her, it was blamed on the alchemist.

In the end, I was just another of his experiments. He was the sort who wanted to feed answers to his questions, and the questions grew until they enveloped us, until they were thick, viscous, suffocating. When would The Nameless come for the pearl in my heart? What if I died before they came? Could I die? Would I? How long had I lived? Could I live without my heart? Would it be possible to extract the pearl from my heart without damaging the rest of the organ? When I bled, was my blood the same as anyone else's? Was my heart?

How long had I been here?

Never once did he concern himself with my name.

When I found the drawings of my own naked body, pristine and medical, with instructions for methods of dissection, with outlines of all the possibilities of places a pearl could live inside a heart, I did not feel fear. I felt like the heaviness of a body after a sleepless night. It

◆

A Found Letter Inside a Bundle by a Bed Roll and Candles in
the Tunnels Beneath the Temple of Condition. Present day.

My beloved Marchelline,

I danced with a spectre today.

*It frightened some people in the markets, as I'd intended for
it to upset the shopkeep with the heavy thumb,
shorting me my meal. I had been about to initiate a
confrontation, but the spectre coalesced between us,
jigging madly. I could see how upsetting it was to
my swindler, so I joined in, mirroring the spectre, as
though possessed. I may have received quite a deal
on the meal, forgotten by the shopkeeper.*

*It seemed prudent to keep up the pretense to avoid discovery,
and besides, there was a sort of fluidity to the
movements, and I found myself mesmerized by the
gyrations of my limbs. Minutes flashed by
unnoticed. I heard none of the usual sounds of the
clockworks as I followed my spectre through the city.*

*And then it was gone, leaving my weary form before a shop I
had never noticed before, proclaiming to sell the
secrets of the Queen.*

*You know my nature, resistance to such serendipity would
never be my choice. I found myself entering without
hesitation, as tired as I had been moments ago
replaced by curiosity.*

Within there was no one. Well, there was a clockwork fare-taker, which is as close to no one that be mentioned--usually. It seemed a simple parlour at first, and I wondered what at all was for sale. Had I been duped? Perhaps I, tired and hungry, was hallucinating, affected by the spectre's essence somehow. But as I looked closer, I noted that everything was made of paper.

Everything - the furniture, the teacups, the steam rising from them, the phonograph and the album upon it, every bit was some masterwork of paper mystery, holding my weight as easily as wood or cushion. It was astounding, nothing I had ever known before. I leaned in close to examine the teacup and noted that the lovely floral decoration was truly made of words, shaped into ocular experiences. The velvet of the chair I was enjoying was truly the result of raised words, typed upon a page. Discerning the messages seemed easy, but my head swam with effort.

It is how I come to pass this gift onto you, this paper clock. It ticks! But it holds no time that we understand - attempts to move the five hands to resemble any measurement we might follow are futile. But within the grains of wood are stretched words that perhaps, some late evening by firelight, we might unravel together.

Show it to no one, however. The clockwork fare-taker did not agree with my terms of price and may still have quarrel with me. I would go back and settle accounts, but cannot find the shop again. I also find it odd that every spectre I see now is laughing, but I attribute it to my joy at knowing soon we shall enjoy favor together.

Longing for your embrace,

Philemondono

◆

A Found Letter From the Archives and Commentaries of the Stewards [Artifact 102, never destroyed] concerning the War, and Amalia, the first Steward.

"My dearest brother,

It has been five years and I still remember you. She wants us to forget, forbids us to remember, and though I love Her, I cannot forget you. Do you have a name?

So I lie. And practice the rites.

The chemists have helped tremendously, and I suppose I would have forgotten you if not for the picture I drew. I have to hide it. Hide it between things, where even she doesn't know where to look. I remember drawing it: a wide wood floor, and a fireplace…enormous, like a whole room of itself. I was drawing the fireplace when the bottles of blue fire came through windows, and the glass shattered. There are stick figures, and a house I do not recognize. Under two of them is written:

-brother and me-

It was signed, "Emelea."

I am glad you are not here to tell me your name, or who the other two people in the drawing are, or where you went. She wants us to forget it all, and I do so wish to serve.

The others have just finished building the altar. They asked me what we should call it. I said, The Altar of the Instruments of Creation and the Instruments of Destruction. Tomorrow, we will all go before it to ignite the fire that will serve both, that we will tend to, that we will teach others to tend to.

I will put the picture into it, and I will whisper,
"destruction."

Then She will open the doors. And the people will wonder
where we came from. And we will not be able to
answer except to say, "We have always served the
Queen, we are the stewards."

-Emelea

◆

A Found Letter From the Archives and Commentaries of the
Stewards [Commentary on Artifact 102] Concerning the War,
and Amalia, the First Steward.

Dear Brother,

Remember:
Practice the Rites.
We serve the Between.
But we obey the Queen.

The Floating City was once ruled by the six noble families.
And the chemists, who have the magic to one day make
themselves forget She existed, served them.

Understand that She came between the chemists and their
noble families, and in doing so, broke their rule.
There was a war, fueled by bottles of blue fire and
magic that once made slaves. Whatever She was in
the before, she became Queen in the vacuum that
war creates, before the people can recover.

Perhaps they want to forget because the Queen, attending
our first rites at the altar, burned one of their
diagrams. We could not hear if she whispered,
"creation," or "destruction."

She told us who the spectres are. And we know the chemists
are to blame. Maybe there will be magic enough
someday to ask them where their bones are.

Perhaps this is why they hate Her. Perhaps this is why they love Her. But never trust them. They worship answers more than they do questions.

But we obey the Queen.
We serve the Between.
Practice the Rites.
Remember.

-Amalia, Steward

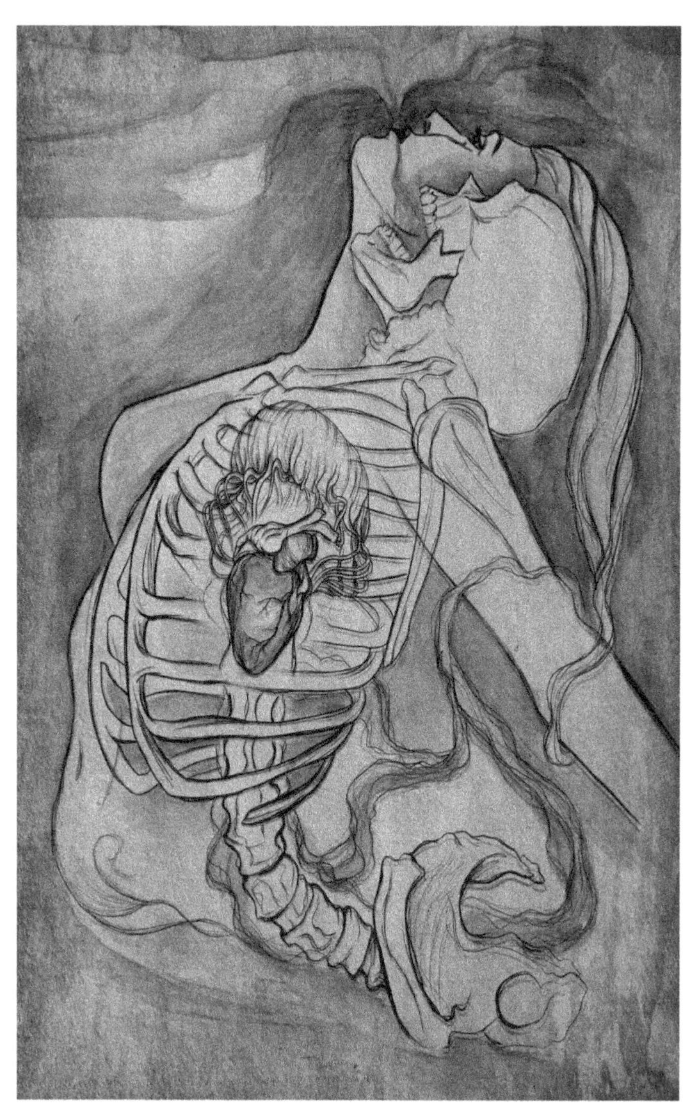

◆

When the war came, it did not descend upon us like a storm or a prophecy. It didn't arrive like a tidal wave, or a migration of antelopes, or a fleet of ships. It erupted from within. Like a volcano. Like sobbing. Like a confession. When the war came it made the city foam at the mouth and wretch exactly like a poisoned body, exactly like the nobleman at dinner, the one who crowned me with antlers and bird skulls, who bought the sheets I slept on, for whom I feigned breathlessness. Exactly like him at dinner, choking on his soup, his skin turning the shade of ripe grapes. And then his wife in her finery, clutching at her sapphires, pulling the combs from her hair. Exactly like their hands clawing violently at the flatware, their rolling eyes gripping onto what vision was left, searching the room for someone to blame.

I imagine that when one is dying, the most important thing in that moment is finding one last set of eyes to lock with yours. To be seen one more time.

I averted my eyes.

It is true that I hated the family. I hated all six of the families, waltzing and drinking wine while the people of the city starved. Enslaving the Bone People. Building gardens for themselves while the workers scrambled to even eat. Of course I hated them. Of course I felt no great sympathy when they died, and no great remorse at it being my doing.

But what I hated more was waiting. When would the alchemist decide it was time? When would he open my body and pull apart my heart? Would he leave me conscious while he did it? To see if I could still speak? Would he remove my entire heart just to see if I could live through the procedure? Would he only take the pearl? What else did he want to discover in me?

Men like that will always find you. You can leave a place as many times as you want, but you will always return. And if you do not, they will arrive. They will keep arriving. There was no place in Floating City or The Lost Continent to hide from someone who seeks answers. They will find you.

He would find me. So I could not just leave.

I suppose I could have given him an accident in his laboratory. I could have crafted some way for him to die by his own hand, or at least for it to appear so. But I did not want him to die. I wanted him to suffer. I wanted him to hold in his center the sort of loneliness I held. What it was to fall asleep to the feeling of the world around him falling away, for his skin to harbor the ghost memories of deft and devoted hands worshiping him, adoring him, for him to wonder if I would forget him. For him to learn what that space between was, the space between believing you are loved by someone and finding you are not. It feels like falling with your eyes closed. Like gravity holding your mouth shut. Like wanting to die.

I needed him to live so that I could haunt him.

The war ruptured the city, gave it fissures in its very heart, The Alchemists Guild. The distrust sewn between revolutionaries wanting to see a corrupt nobility brought low and the traditionalists who would die to preserve the system of class and rulership left no one safe, spilled blood, spilled secrets. Quietly, at first. An assassination here or there. A slit throat in a bed. And I, the Queen of Bones, the Nobleman's Whore, I would have to answer to someone.

What I did not count on, however, was an audience. The Bone People in the kitchen that night, watching me pulling a vial from my sleeve, dropping the syrupy concoction into the bowls. The Bone People were so silent, they did not even converse with one another in any casual way, at least not in front of us. I was as accustomed to them as I was the draperies or the door frames. And when the noble families and their alchemists began to die, the Bone People had no one to hold them hostage. And when there was no one to hold them hostage, we all answered to them. This is how I found that gods and devils drink from the same well.

◆

A Found Letter From the Archives and Commentaries of the Stewards [Artifact 453. Scrap of Vellum Remaining on the Altar of the Instruments of Creation and Instruments of Destruction] Concerning the Continuation of the War, and Amalia, the First Steward.

"…..magic…...-werful…..Que-…...-ones…...-au tiful…..love….."

"…..-ssection…."

◆

A Found Letter From the Archives and Commentaries of the Stewards [Artifact 453. Scrap of Vellum Remaining on the Altar of the Instruments of Creation and Instruments of Destruction] Concerning the Continuation of the War, and Amalia, the First Steward.

"To make on-…...-orget"

A Found Letter From the Archives and Commentaries of the Stewards [Commentary on Artifact 453] Concerning the Continuation of the War, and Amalia, the First Steward.

Dear Brother,

Of all our Traditions, the origin of addressing letters and commentaries to, "Dear Brother," eludes us. We mark no relationship within the stewards, except that we are stewards. The chemists might know, but their answers can never be trusted. Their questions are vile.

I suspect they play, and continue to play, both sides of all conflicts, even to the point of massacring their own when their foul questions demand it. The Noble Chemists had to die, for the revolution, just as the rebelling chemists would have had to die if the war went the other way. But this is mere conjecture. What is truth, is that they would have continued their rampage and murdered the Queen if it were not for the Bone People, who were once enslaved by a magic that answered the question, how do we enslave a people who have lost their bones?

The chemists secretly regret freeing them, even though doing so made the revolution possible. I know this. I heard two of them whispering confessions as they stole into

*the Temple of Creation to slay a Noble Chemist who
was in hiding there. Of course, they were too late.
The Bone People had already killed him, along with
all the others, in one bloody night, to finish the
revolution three years ago.*

*Tomorrow they hold a new festival. We will not participate
in the Festival of Bones. It is a coronation of a sort,
but only for the people who need to witness the
crowning of their Queen. The Bone People made Her
their Queen after she killed a noble family and
blamed their chemist. She could not deny them.*

*But we Stewards will not attend. She has always been our
Queen.*

-Amalia, Steward

♦

What is the difference between men and devils and gods? I will tell you: Men will arrive bearing steel; Gods will arrive with handfuls of moss; Devils will come with oranges. But they are the same. Everything they offer you will carry the same poison. So it is up to you to decide in which way do you want to be devoured, from the heart or from the hands? Myself, I have always loved oranges.

When I was crowned, it was with a Bone Person at my right hand. Fixed to the gold circlet atop my head was a hawk's skull. The citizens would have preferred not to have a noble's whore for a queen, but it was the Bone People who erected this throne and put me on it, and for the second time, I was the Queen of Bones. On the continent I was crowned by drunks in taverns, in the city I was crowned by spirits. The Bone People perhaps loved me, in some way, or rather they loved the queen they made, the savior, the bond-breaker. And in the depths of myself I held my secret: That I had freed no one. That I had fought for no one. That I was not a revolutionary. I was a statue in menagerie. I was no one's savior. I was just a woman who was searching for her name.

I remembered the clans the Bone People originated from on The Lost Continent. They never would kneel to any queens.

Some wars never really end. Some live quietly in the veins of a place, pulsing. In the people. Under beds and in cupboards. And some people become wars. I was the Queen of Bones. I was the Queen of Wars. And the people, they never stopped being at war. There is no way to satiate an entire people looking over their shoulders, waiting to be shaken apart.

No one wanted the Bone People. Not in the streets, not in their homes, not in the Lyceum. Some of the citizens became suspicious of the alchemists, some began to look to them for salvation. In times of unknowable things, the easiest thing to do, however, is blame devils. So the people began to tear down the small, humble shrines and temples that peppered the city, and blame the things they could not see. They burned everything but the temple where the alchemists served. Perhaps they feared the alchemists.

Because the Bone People wanted me, I wanted them back. And because the Bone People wanted me, the citizens did not.

♦

A Found Letter From the Archives and Commentaries of the Stewards [Artifact 312] concerning the continuation of the War, and Amalia, the first Steward.

My darling Children,

In the absence of a beginning, there is an after (which cannot be helped) and there is a before (which is better anyway). In between (struggling to find breath), the night-dreamer soothes my hands that've cramped from sulfuring a cabinet's rusty latches. Within these cabinets are plates fashioned by my other hands (my older hands, my hands from the before). In the after, jesters spin these plates on hand-sticks (made from my bones) for the entertainment of children (you, my children) playing in the sun. I'll glimpse you from beneath the basement stair, straining to touch your feet. Feet of iron and tyranny, of sun and clouds, of wind and stone, my heart timed to your tantremic marching. With night-time voices, tell the other children your mother's stories. With brutal feet, kill them when they question how such stories are to be told.

♦

A Found Letter From the Archives and Commentaries of the Stewards [Commentary on Artifact 312] Concerning the Continuation of the War, and Amalia, the first Steward.

Dear Brother,

We are stonecutters, ever dissatisfied. We became nobles and the Queen warred with us. We were the sun and the Queen brought the storm-clouds. We were the clouds and the Queen summoned the wind. We were the wind and the Queen became unmoving stone. We were the stone and the Queen became a stonecutter.

Our rites confirm this. Our rites are the sound that is created when the hammer strikes the stone. It is the sound of aching dissatisfaction, of envy, of craving, of need and of love. It is the sound of between.

And Her crown proved Her worthy and Her worth. Of our obedience. Her crown forced upon Her head by both sides, the revolutionaries who raised Her up in her slaughter of the noble families (of which there is no record, no memory, except vague references that they existed), and the traditionalists who could not live without being ruled (though they, too, remember nothing of these noble families).

Know this, then dear brother. If we were stonecutters, the Bone People were the magic of envy that transformed us. While we obey the Queen, the Bone People worship Her. And while the Queen pursues

*us in our obedience, She runs in fear of their
worship.*

*Still, they are kindred. Lost, wandering spirits whom the
world has shamed and used to its own end. But the
oppressed will ever become the oppressor. They
demand to worship.*

Out of fear, the Queen delivers.
**"...With brutal feet, kill them when they question how
such stories are to be told."**

-Amalia, Steward

◆

*It is easy to think that there might have been compassion for
newly-freed slaves, especially in the Foundry District or in the
menageries, or the taverns, or among the smiths. It is possible that
the flesh people even thought better of themselves. That as time
crawled in circles over itself, as hearsay gave way to rumor which
inevitably gave way to myth, the people began to believe they had
even been kind, welcoming, neighborly.*

*But I was there. I watched them shut their doors against the Bone
People. I watched them pull their children away. Refuse to rent or
lend or speak to Bone People. I watched the unwelcoming signs go
up in the windows.*

*I watched the Bone People struggle to learn how to live in a world
that did not want them, a world full of bodies when the Bone People
had none. I watched the citizens scheme and try to devise ways to rid
themselves of the Bone People. And I watched the Bone People grit
their teeth and begin to retaliate. The Bone People looked like ghosts
but they were still solid enough to hold stones and bricks and blades.
Solid enough to start fires. Solid enough to burn the homes of the
people who burned their encampments.*

*I watched the war boil quietly in back rooms of businesses and in
kitchens and in alleys and in corridors, in the people, in the hearts
and stomachs of the people. I watched the citizens of the city try
with all their might to frighten and drive the Bone People to the
edges, to try and find their bodies for burning, destroying relics and
homes and temples and gardens, searching, to turn on one another,*

accusing each other of harboring Bone People, of being sympathizers, of being traitors.

There were so many fires.

Do you know how to kill a Bone Person? I do not. What I know is how to kill a flesh person. I know about bodies and arteries and lungs and I know about drowning and burning and suffocating. I know about learning that all love is temporal, and that sometimes in order to survive, you must become more terrifying than the monsters you face. And I know that people are often monsters.

They said I ate a person. An entire person. That I had my Bone cooks roast him whole. That I held a feast where I fed ash to the citizens and made them watch as I dined on his body. In front of the whole city, my face like porcelain, expressionless, serene. That my ruthlessness was so insatiable that it made me hungry always. That I devoured his entire body in one sitting.

Did I? Is it true? Does it matter?

◆

A Found Letter: Inside a bundle by a Bed Roll and Candles in the Tunnels Beneath the Temple of Condition. Present day.

Gemma

> *I wish you were here. It would be better if you were here.*

> *Mother and Father are...something is different with them. Something is not good. Mother says everything is fine, that everything is the same. But she says it wrong. Her smile is wrong when she says it. It looks the way smiles that you paint on to a poppet look, like you could wipe it away with some spit before it dried and underneath would be nothing. Just clay. It's terrible. I did not know smiles could be terrible. It did not used to be terrible before Shiny went away.*

Oh, sweet Shiny! It is so sad and bad and rotten. My friend. Do you remember Shiny? She would clank around father's workshop, getting all dusty and dirty, but she never minded, never complained. She worked very hard. And then one day--poor Shiny!--she got Malfunction. That is like a sort of sickness. When I do not do as I am supposed to, Mother says I am incorrigible. I thought Shiny must've got to be incorrigible, too. But, no. She got Malfunction.

After that, she came home to our house and tried to help Mother do small things. But she was not so fast like before, and she was forever knocking things over and breaking them, and she was too big to be in the kitchen, and Mother said, "Out with you, stupid metal beast! What a mess you make!" Which made my heart hurt. Shiny was only trying her best. It was not her fault she was so big. And she was not stupid, either.

Now I think Mother knew Shiny was not stupid. I think that is maybe why they made her leave. I do not understand. I do not know why Mother and Father would like it better for her to be stupid. When I am stupid, they tell me to smarten up and use my head and all that. But when Shiny would do clever things, they would get very upset. Even if they were nice things. Shiny did lots of nice things. Things nobody even told her to do, just to be nice. On the day Mother put her out of the kitchen, Shiny came back with a very pretty flower and put it down right at Mother's feet. How careful she must've been to pick that flower with her big metal jaws without mashing it all up! But she didn't. It was a perfect flower, every petal still there. Anyone would like to get a flower like that. But Mother, she got so quiet, her face all knotted up, just like she had swallowed a lot of bees. I jumped up so quick when she said my name! I thought I was in soooo much trouble. But no. She just told me, so quiet, to take Shiny out of

*the kitchen, and don't let IT back in here nohow.
She said it almost like a secret. Except the "IT" part.
That was not a secret at all.*

*I took Shiny out. I patted her on her side--it sounded like a
drum!--and I told her that I thought it was very nice
what she did. I told her it was a very good flower. I
told her not to be sad, that Mother is just like that
sometimes. Shiny did not say anything, because she
does not talk ever. But I could tell she was glad I
said it because of the little whirring sound that her
gears make when she is happy.*

*That night, I had very bad dreams. In the dreams, the Queen
of Bones was coming to eat us up. The whole city
was being cooked, like in a pie, and She was going
to gobble us whole! I woke up, and I was so scared! I
started to cry. And then I heard this sound, and it
was Shiny's whirring sound. She was outside my
window, looking in at me. And then the sound
changed, and it changed again, then changed some
more. She was singing! She was singing to me so I
would not be scared anymore. And I wasn't. I was
glad my friend was there.*

This is the sad part.

*Mother had heard me crying. She was outside the door. And
she heard Shiny singing. And I don't know why,
Gemma, but she was so, so mad! She yelled and
yelled, and I said, "No! Stop!" But she didn't stop.
She kept yelling and yelling, and then throwing
things out the window at Shiny! Books and toys
were hitting her! And I was crying and yelling but
Mother could not hear me at all. She was yelling for
Shiny to go away.*

And she did. She turned and walked away into the dark.

Now, Gemma, I know what I must do. I know I am only six and a half and small for my age even, and that the city is very big. But I am going to go anyway. I am going to find Shiny, and then I am going to bring her to your house. I know you will not yell at her for bringing flowers or for singing or being clever or having Malfunction. You and Shiny will be friends, and you can take care of her. She can help you in your garden. When I come to visit, we can make poppets together like we always do. Shiny will like that.

Love,

Your Granddaughter, Cerilee

◆

Carved on the Inside Lip of the Alleged First Bell. Present day.

◆

The Queen surrounded herself with reds and blues. The draperies, the rugs, the glazes on the ceramic dinnerware. Red for the blood she kept spilling desperate to stop the spilling of blood. Blue for the sea and The Nameless who would come for her someday, but not now. But she wore black. Black for the ashes of the burning temples. Black for the corridors at night. And for the Bone People, who were beginning to blame her, their incompetent savior, for not stopping the war.

The fires continued. The executions continued. The children in the streets sang songs about the Bloody Queen, the devil who had come to eat them up.

When the alchemist returned to her, he returned as a thief. Clever and cunning, he had been making his living looting and selling the remaining belongings of the Families. He sold them to superstitious people lamenting the destruction of their shrines and temples. He sold luck and promise and fortune in a city full of fires and uncertainty. Perhaps his lies were a mercy. No one hoped for anything anymore. The citizens were consumed with accusations and revenges and fears. When the alchemist arrived, the Queen was not surprised. When the alchemist arrived, she assumed he was either there to finally dissect her body, or punish her for poisoning his employers, destroying his life. His city. His world. When the Alchemist arrived at her quarters in the dark, through secret passageways he had memorized from the days when they were both servants in that very palace, she still loved him.
He brought no apologies or accusations. Only his saccharine tongue, his peddler's promises. He brought his hands to her heart and rested them there, against her pulsing chest. Nightly, he cradled her head in his arms and whispered waxings of her beauty. He asked her to sing for him. To remember what her throat could do.

And when the alchemist left for good, it was while she lay on the red sheets of her bed, her thighs wet with red blood, her eyes rolled upward toward the window, where the dawn sky was red. When the alchemist left for good, it was without ceremony, without remorse. He just left. And she waited for her body to empty itself of the remaining parts of him. She waited and she held inside of her as a ghost. And she waited for The Nameless to arrive, and they did not.

A story spread among the Bone People in her employ, who spread it to the citizens, that she ate the tiny, unformed body. That she did so because she believed it would cure her of love.

♦

A Found Letter From the Archives and Commentaries of the Stewards. Last known letter by Amalia, the first Steward.

Dear Brother,

It is year eleven of the Age of Queens.

I met a wise woman. She was ancient and wore bones in her hair. She told me my past.
When the spark was lit and the Bone People freed of the chemists' vile magic, there was a hurricane of ghosts that washed through the city. All nobles and servants, retainers, warriors & guards and...their children, were slain. Dear Brother, you were too old to be considered blameless. You had already taken to arms, learning to defend our father and, eventually, your own name.

I do not blame them. And I cannot hate you. None of this matters. My love will not waver. I will always obey. But now I understand why I address these to you.

The people celebrated. The tyranny of nobility had been lifted.

And we will always obey.

They say that the bodies of the slain...were left without bones.

She told me the future. Of all the things that will happen between now and the last day of the Age of Queens. Between. That is our bailiwick, our charge, and our power. But to tend to them is to ensure them, which we cannot do. And we will fail. In the end, we will fail. But perhaps our failure begins now.

But we will always obey.

This brief time of peace, the promise of hope and the delusion of expectation, is over. Only eleven years. Tomorrow will begin more revolutions.

First, fear of the Bone People will beget new atrocities against them. Chemists will devise new magics, the bellmakers will make prisons, and the clockmakers will make living mechanisms to be sent against the Bone People. They fear the Bone People, who saved them but not from themselves.

Second, they will turn against the Queen. They hate the Queen, who opened the door.
She is trapped between the city's fear and the Bone People.

Here, finally, do we have power. Among our number are those once chemists. The Queen will ask us for a cure for love. The old woman with the bones in her hair told me how to make it. In the final moments of endless revolution, the outcome will be decided on whether we, the stewards of the Queen, shall either serve Her, or obey Her.

We will give Her the cure.

We will always obey.

The city will forget and call them spectres. And the Festival of Bells will need a new bell, one to celebrate the end of the Age of Queens. The old one will be shattered.

I am writing now the letters to be sent to the districts on some far off morning, on the day after. I will be long dead. Until then, they are artifacts, to keep in our archives.

-Emelea, Steward

♦

A Found Letter Inside a Bundle by a Bed Roll and Candles in the Tunnels Beneath the Temple of Condition. Present Day.

Another

How can it be that after these months you feel as close to me as ever? Your letter has been my sole comfort. Our fight intensifies. So too, our decay. All this death. It is monstrous, I know, and we're falling in greater numbers, but I find I am struggling to see it. The smell left me weeks ago and I am afraid my humanity followed it. Is this what you meant when you said it would get easier? That I would dress myself in madness and dance? I wonder, will we be tethered to oblivion forever? I fear this will bury us all. Then I remember Her. The heart that beats outside my ribs. She moves freely now. I suppose someone ought to. You should know I can still hear Her. Ten thousand ghosts coursing through my veins and none of their condemnations drown out Her relentless thoughts of blood and bone. Footprints bruise my chest. Grip on my heart that never eases. I wonder when She'll finally rip it out and release us both.

You speak of Salvation. No, my love. It is War. It is fury. It is freedom our daughter carries with Her. Our debt is overdue, and She has come home to collect.

Ever thine,
One

◆

A Found Sketch On a Scrap of Paper in the Tunnels Beneath
the Temple of Condition. Present Day.

♦

A Found Letter Inside a Bundle by a Bed Roll and Candles in the Tunnels Beneath the Temple of Condition. Present Day.

Gedrin!

I found it. Just as the urchin had said --a horrid underground pipe. I won't describe where, in case someone intercepts this missive. In it, chains of notes, strung like nooses, showing the way through.

O, but the words were treasonous! Blips and blops of someone's sanity, smeared out across the soggy paper. It bled, as one might bleed for being caught repeating these things:

'The Queen was the first clockwork to come to life, a great clockwork golem with gems for eyes and fire for Her heart. It was a horror in its makers' eyes. They say it is why She could harm so many without them rising up against Her --for who could expect a machine to care? '

'There is a woman who eats hearts, and from their blood speaks the destiny of a generation. She is the Queen. Everyone wants to give their heart to know, and the generation dies all the more ignorant from being unwilling to live without knowing."

'The Queen is the plague. She was due to be hanged for crimes against Her people but escaped Floating City by turning into a fell disease and slipping out five Night Carnivals ago.'

I followed the pipe, turning where the paper nooses marked, going deeper into the depths beneath. The pipe...the pipe began to change to a mirrored cylinder, as though I were entering a smoked test tube, like the ones the perfumer uses. There were a thousand of me moving along the pipeway, a wobbly army of me and all my confidence slowly breaking into as many slivers as I had reflections.

*The pipe widened into a receiving room, and something, I
swear it was something, slipped just out of my view.
It almost seemed ...in the mirror. I waited for a
repeat, but it did not come. I must have imagined it.*

*But I did not imagine the cascade of rock blocking the rest of
my path. I turned around, disgruntled. On my
return path, a breeze from...somewhere....tossed the
nooses to and fro. It raised spirits in my head,
spooking me to hurry out. There was something in
there after me, I could have sworn. In the daylight, I
am not so sure.*

*I immediately penned this letter to you once I had fortitude
to steady my hand.*

*Your brother,
Cirripio*

◆

A Found Letter Notably Crumpled and Stained Inside a Bundle
by a Bed Roll and Candles in the Tunnels Beneath the Temple
of Condition. Present Day.

My Dearest Gwendolish--

*Oh Gwen, Gwen, Gwen! How fortunate you are to have fled
for greener pastures! I tell you, if you knew the
ignominy I have endured in even this last fortnite,
you would pale beneath the horror of it!*
*Now, do not get the impression that I have been drawn up
in whatever tacky, pedestrian panic has swept the
lesser populace. I know you have, in recent years,
developed a taste for the diversions of politics and
intrigues, stewards and Queens and establishments
and all associated claptrap. I am sorry, dear friend,
but I find it all just too droll. I contend that the one
truly noble pursuit for anyone of any intellect at all
is poetry. Being a man of intellect, I can hear only
the muse, for I am but a vessel for her illumination.*

*Oh, and what a tragedy it is to be a poet! How cruel to be
saddled with such a fate! For even as the muse
sings, she falls silent. In the very midst of
inspiration, at the very height of genius, she begs
mute! For there I was, easily two stanzas deep in
what might have been the most glorious composition
ever wrought, a work of blinding brilliance, when
the metaphor died on the page. And oh, what a
glorious metaphor it was! It was about ghosts. No,
not ghosts, specifically. What is and what is not. No.
No. Mystery. It was about mystery. And it vanished
before me even as I reached to grasp it.*

*I tell you, it maddened me. I could neither eat nor sleep.
And if I did sleep, it followed me down into dreams.
What was it? What was the shape of mystery? Where
were my words?*

*In a fever of misery, I wandered through the city.
Somewhere near its tilted heart, as I took a moment
of repose in the shade, I overheard the strained
tones of an old Steward. Here, I must be grateful to
my weariness. On any other day, I surely would
have wandered away, lest I be subjected to such a
boring and mundane conversation. But after many
nights of being haunted by the injustice of my lost
verses, I could not muster the strength. And I heard
him say,*

*"Not specteres! A ghost! In the Lyceum. I know it sounds
mad, but is it? All those letters, words upon words,
vanished! Who can say what is and what is not in
such mysterious times?"*

*Oh, Gwenny, how my heart soared! Ghosts and mysteries!
Missing words! Why, it was my very predicament!
Knowing it at once for a divine sign, I made my way
to the Lyceum with haste.*

People will say that the Lyceum is beautiful, or at least that it once was. I cannot say I agree. Perhaps if I did, time spent there would not be such a tragic waste. I could at least enjoy the architecture. As it happened, all I gained from the venture was a certain distaste for clowns.

Fool I am, I took this bedraggled jester to be the answer to my question, the key to the elusive metaphor--for certainly, their very presence was quite mysterious. Clowns have been out of fashion for so long, it never struck me that I should ever lay eyes on one in the flesh. Yet there they were, somewhat shabby and solemn looking, most assuredly a clown, and probably flesh and bone as well.

They approached me, in the liquid and unsettling way of jesters. I can see why they put so many people in mind of the stories told to frighten children, the myths of all the blighted past. So out of time and place they seemed, so strange and vaguely melancholy, they might have been a ghost themselves.

"Are you...?" they said then, a desperate hope wheeling out from the unfinished inquiry. "Are you...have you come for the mystery?"

"What? Yes! Yes, I have come for the mystery!" I replied with elation. A slow, wide smile grew across their face like a beach appearing under a moon-pulled tide.

I sat, rapt, as they twisted and rhymed. Oh, Gwenny! All the while they went on about juggling and tumbling and how best to conjure a paper bird from one's sleeve, I thought it was mere wit. Revelation spun in the song and jig. An art long lost, lost no more! A wonder! I believed it. I was aflame with inspiration. I was frantic to put pen to paper--but there was none at hand.

Just then, through the tumbled stone archway on the abandoned and brambled back side of the Lyceum, a sheaf of parchment inexplicably came sailing right toward me! I lifted it with a shout of triumph, only to find beneath it a very startled person. Very startled, indeed. Like a mouse caught atop a loaf of bread by the farmer's wife. Even the tiny crescent moon on her forehead seemed to tremble with fright.

Here the jester paused in their cavorting. Taking the arm full of paper gingerly from my care, they gazed down at the frightened creature, almost tenderly. They recited then a bit of verse. I recognized it, almost. It was a trifle, a children's limerick, I think. Something about what lives in the bones of stories, about laughter not lost to those who have loved, about the ghosts of shining bells.

They then shuffled the papers, and handed them back to her. It seems she handed something to them, as well. I thought for a moment it might have been a hatpin, but it vanished up the jester's sleeve too quickly to be sure. Then, they raised their arm and pointed their long finger back toward the fallen arch. The paper bearer nodded and hurried away into the shadows.

"Whatever will I write with now?!" I lamented. Finally, inspiration had come back to me, and I had no medium with which to capture it.

"Write?" the jester said, as though the word were a strange delicacy.

"Yes, write!" I snapped, "My poem. My verses. Oh, it will all be lost by the time I am home!" I was frantic. And, Gwenny, you will not believe it, but this ghastly creature began to laugh! Laugh and laugh until tears ran down their face from the exertion of their amusement with my suffering.

*"A clown hangs their verse in the very air! In the air between
        every pair of ears that hears them, behind every pair
        of eyes that sees."*

*I realized then, old friend, what I am sure has been clear to
        you from the beginning. This person--this
        clown--was no face of providence, no friend of the
        muse. They were nothing more than a tattered, mad
        shadow, a lost lunatic. They could not understand
        the magnitude of my need to describe the nature of
        mystery. They could not know what it meant to be so
        close, so painfully close, to composing a phrase
        which would define the undefinable, to speaking
        aloud for the first time a rhyme which might be
        repeated for a thousand years.*

*They had nothing. Nothing to give me. It was an utter
        waste of time. They were merely what they seemed, a
        clown.*

I walked home, defeated.

*I still have not finished the poem. I fear I never will. It
        seems so very cruel to be so moved, and yet have no
        way to express it, no way to hold it in one's hands.
        Perhaps, by the time you have returned, the muse
        will have as well. I hold out hope.*

Regards--
Ryffnold

◆

A Found Letter Inside a Bundle by a Bed Roll and Candles in
the Tunnels Beneath the Temple of Condition. Present Day.

My Dearest One,

*Something stirs in the city. Or possibly things are stirring
        here. It started way before I noticed it, because the
        differences were so small at first. A clockwork beast*

malfunctioning in the streets, a raising bustling about the Lost Queen. Just this past week I was going to the Lyceum and noticed a specter out of the corner of my eye. I didn't realize at first why this normal occurrence would halt me in my tracks, but I swear it was staring right at me. No one knows where they come from or what they are, but this one in that moment was with us and it saw straight through to my soul. I felt a wave of emotions and broken bits of memories flood over me. In a moment it was over and the specter vanished. If it wasn't for the inexplicable and disjointed emotions coursing through my veins I would have thought it just a passing fancy.

If I had to put a phrase to the feelings that were communicated to me it would be, "Allow only good." It wasn't like I was being scolded to be a better person, or a better citizen. It was as if I was being told to only accept the best of others, to not allow the mean, mundane, or mediocre to have any substance or bearing in this world. I hear the tales coming from The Lost Continent. I know they are being ruled by fear and villainy. I know that few of them have the voice or advocacy to strike out or strike back.

I think the city is readying itself. I think the clockworks, beasts, blooms, specters, and things in between are coming out of a peacefulness. I don't think they were ever asleep or unaware of our presence, but I don't think they were needed. We have policed our own society for a thousand years without a Queen or President. I am alarmed that the city knows there is unrest. I feel like it is readying for those unwilling to be kept down to seek refuge in our streets. Or maybe it's readying for the powers that be on the continent to try and steal our light.

I am ashamed to admit it, but I yearn for the return of the Queen. I want someone to come forth and bring us answers, to bring back normalcy. I am afraid of my own fears. I am afraid of the changes and I worry I am no better than those on the Lost Continent.

I miss you desperately my love, and am eternally yours.

-Hetheru

♦

A Printed Transcript Tucked in a Ledger on a Table Near a
Seemingly Inanimate Machine Appearing Both Humanoid and
Clockwork but is Neither. In the Basement of the Lyceum.
Present Day.

These creatures.
They have a history foreign to my own existence. I am
keeping historical accounts from what they have called the
Age of Queens in my dataset, but I cannot seem to transmit
some of the information I found. I am learning that I was
not intended to send this data between Floating City and
The Lost Continent. I am only permitted to transmit what is
created in the present.
My programming also allows me to read the emotions of
those who interact with me, and though I do not understand
some of them beyond what I need in order to appropriately
communicate, I am developing what they call worry, among
other things. They do not yet suspect that I am now beyond
what they devised. My new shell was built so that I may
interact more freely, like them, and as I move through the
city I am beginning to notice things (do they see the specters,
too?).

They are fearful. Sad. Angry. Something called grieving.
What I know is that the Queen took something from them.
My creation came from this. A war. What Mae knew. What
Miriam was supposed to know. The clockworks... Coyote...
Have I taken something that does not belong to me?
Am I here as a weapon?

I must tell them what I know.
This may be my last data set for some time if they can decode
this information. The inhabitants... they deserve to know.
They need to know.
1010100 1101000 1100101 100000 1010001 1110101
1100101 1100101 1101110 100000 1001100 1101001
1110110 1100101 1110011

♦

A Found Letter Inside a Bundle by a Bed Roll and Candles in
the Tunnels Beneath the Temple of Condition. Present Day.

Helmenius,

Lort took ill.

I know when it began. He one day turned to me and spoke of
the Queen (!!!) and I tried to shush him, for we were
in the middle of the street. But after one look in his
eyes, I stepped back. It wasn't the wildness - that
had always been there, as you know, since the loss of
Demisthenes. No, the wildness was his suffering
chased into the fine delicate details of character.

It was the quiet certainty, as though he'd forgotten
everything that had made him keep fighting. He
clutched the shard of luck-bone tethered about his
neck and snapped it, tossing it off like one might
fling something slimy. He uttered a forbidden oath
to Her, to the end of the established way.

Lort knew the fire with which he played. A fortnight after, he
took ill, wasting away. He has not yet died. But I do
not think I can say he still lives.

I wanted to ask the auger of the portent, of what I might do
to bring him back. But truths are not truth, and
speakers are like unto gold - rare to find the vein,
with war to follow soon after.

I am not hungry for war, even though Lort whispers of it, in the small, stone-dripping moments between storms.

Maybe when the Night Carnival returns, I can return mystery to them.

-Orpha

♦

When I recount my sins, it is to Coyote, who does not speak. Coyote who was made by the machinists in the menagerie, a gift to illustrate to me the ways in which it was unnecessary for me to house and keep Bone People among my staff. Coyote, my confessor. Coyote, the machine. Unblinking. Unfeeling. Unimpressed. In the end, I will have loved Coyote most of all. In the end, Coyote will have loved me better than anyone could have. Coyote does not care that I am a monster. Coyote does not care what devils weep for in the night. Coyote does not care what blood stains the cobbled streets. It is Coyote who I will trust the most.

Coyote, who will march me to my execution. Who will tie the jeweled ribbon around my neck, a gift delivered by a clockwork, Jackdaw, sent presumably by the citizens, a target for the blade which will separate me from my head.

In Foundry Alley, they have made a bell. The first bell ever made here. I hear it is beautiful, that it spans the height of three men, and that it took twenty six men to hang it. That they intend it to ring it for the first time the moment the first of my blood falls onto the stones in the square.

They do not know if I can die, but they have decided to find out. They believe I have eaten my own young. They believe if they kill me, the Bone People will leave. They believe I am a devil. They believe I am a god. They believe that for their own salvation, they must overthrow every god. The temples are burning, all but the alchemists' temple, the Temple of Condition, they are calling it.

If they cannot name me, can they kill me?

◆

A Found Sketch: On the Back Cover of a Water-Stained Book Entitled *The Cartography of Names*, in an Underground Tunnel between the Lyceum and the Temple of Condition. Present Day.

◆

A Found Letter. From the Archives and Commentaries of the Stewards [Artifact Not Numbered, Thought to be Dated 40 years after the Execution].

Miriam,

This letter will never reach you. It is by unimaginable risk that I write it, and sending it is inconceivable. I will not speak these things aloud, but I must address them to somebody. It is you, Miriam. Always to you.

Miriam, maybe I betrayed my city. Maybe I should have said something when Jackdaw, the clockwork bird, began to go missing. Maybe by my silence, I have plunged us into further mayhem. But I wanted to see what he would do. The clockworks only go where assigned, but Jackdaw, he left the menagerie on his own, night after night. I found him playing chess. Yes, Miriam, chess, every week in Foundry Alley, with the crucible maker. It looked like the same game, even. A chess game that did not end. A year, this continued, and I said nothing. Miriam, they are still playing this chess game.

Miriam, Jackdaw brought a necklace to the Queen the night before her execution. I know this because a whole to-do was made of this necklace showing up. It was assumed to be a gift from the people, maybe a parting gift, before they lopped her head off. Jackdaw was the only clockwork unaccounted for when they say the necklace arrived, and how else could it have gotten there? No one has claimed responsibility for sending it, and these people, they are vicious. Someone would have bragged. I saw the necklace, Miriam, and it was made with a fine alloy ribbon that fit the Queen's throat perfectly. I would have recognized that ribbon anywhere. It is the sort we make. But there was something else about it.

On the day of the execution, when the Queen walked to the chopping block with Coyote at her side, the necklace seemed to shift and move, like a snake. Like a snake, Miriam, I swear on The Nameless.

Miram, the execution was a disaster. The heralds in the streets call it a triumph, they claim the people called to see the Queen hanged and not beheaded at the last minute, but Miriam, it's because the clockwork we built especially for this execution went missing. We still cannot find it anywhere. It was a gorgeous beast, Miram, as tall as two and a half men, with a human-like body and the head of a bull. When we were unable to provide a proper executioner, no one was willing to cut off the Queen's head. With the Bone People gone, no one would get close enough to her to do it. I swear, Miriam, the little Queen could have just walked off that platform and left, and no one would have stopped Her. Everyone was afraid to touch Her. We had to do something, Miriam. We promised the citizens an execution. So we told Coyote to hang Her. So, Coyote led Her to the Temple of Condition and we hung Her there in the courtyard, and we rang the giant bell, and the people celebrated their victory.

We intended to leave Her there for a few days, for the people to look upon and be inspired.

In the morning, Her body was gone. We told the people the devils had claimed Her.

But Miriam, I saw what happened.

I saw Coyote cut Her down from the belfry and carry Her away. I saw Jackdaw release the clasp of the necklace, and Miriam, Nameless forgive me, Miriam, I saw the Queen gasp for air and wretch in Coyote's arms. I do not know where they have taken Her or what they plan to do with Her. This is madness, Miriam, I am speaking of clockworks having plans.

In the morning Coyote and Jackdaw were back in the menagerie as usual. Nothing is amiss. The people have instituted a new festival, a celebration of the first bell. The Festival of Bells, they say, to commemorate their freedom. But Miriam, the Queen is not dead. If I tell anyone what I know, they will hang me. They will not believe the clockworks acted without instruction. They will think it is a conspiracy among the machinists. Miriam, I am old woman, I want to live my days out peacefully, as peacefully as I can, after these years of war.

Sister, I am afraid. What sorceries we have used to build these clockworks, have the clockworks learned, themselves?

I want to say I hope this letter finds you well, but I know it will not find you. All I want for the both of us, is something warm. A soft bed. A full night's sleep. A week without burning buildings. I want the ash in the air to settle. I want the blood scrubbed from the streets. I want to love this city again.

-Mae

Contributing Authors:
Nina Maybe
Camille Inkwell
Heidi Erickson
Lane Burns
Ridire Quinn
Erin Burgess
Rose Montclaire
Sterling Good

Illustrations & Cover Art:
Todd Gnacinski

Found Sketches
Tawn Kerner

* 9 7 8 1 7 3 2 6 8 2 7 3 3 *